Pinocchio

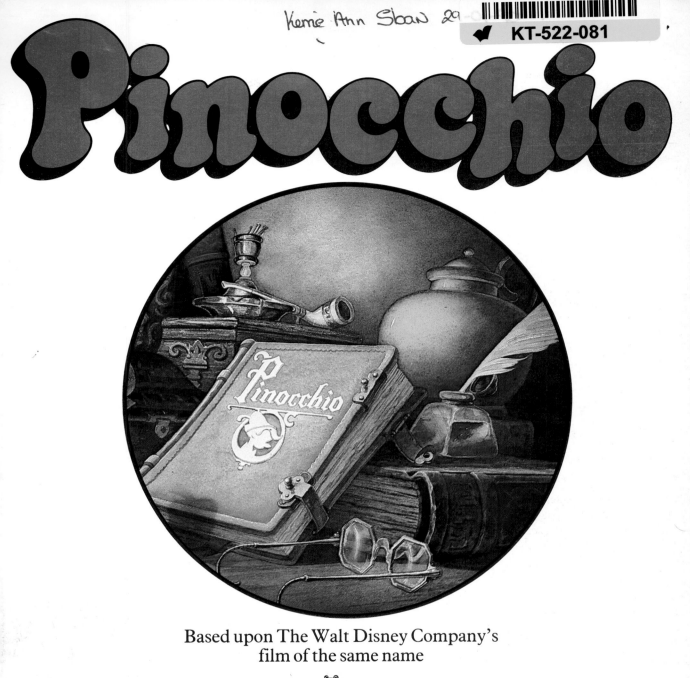

Based upon The Walt Disney Company's
film of the same name

Hippo Books
Scholastic Publications Limited
London

Scholastic Publications Ltd.,
10 Earlham Street, London WC2H 9LN, UK

Scholastic Inc.,
730 Broadway, New York, NY 10003, USA

Scholastic Tab Publications Ltd.,
123 Newkirk Road, Richmond Hill,
Ontario L4C 3G5, Canada

Ashton Scholastic Pty. Ltd.,
PO Box 579, Gosford, New South Wales,
Australia

Ashton Scholastic Ltd.,
165 Marua Road, Panmure, Auckland 6,
New Zealand

This edition first published by Scholastic Publications Limited, 1986 by
arrangement with The Walt Disney Company
Copyright © 1986 The Walt Disney Company

ISBN 0 590 70623 3

Reprinted 1988
All rights reserved
Made and printed by Mateu Cromo, Madrid
Typeset in Plantin by Keyline Graphics, London NW6

In a little village high in the mountains of Italy lived an old
woodcarver called Gepetto. He was all alone in the world,
except for his pet cat Figaro and his pet goldfish Cleo.

  Jiminy Cricket had been travelling for some days when he
came to the village. He looked in through Gepetto's window.
He liked the look of the bright lamplight, and the crackling
fire, and decided this was where he'd spend the night. He
crept under the door, and looked around. On a work bench
was a newly-made wooden boy puppet. Jiminy watched as
Gepetto finished painting it.

"Now," Gepetto said as he put down his brush, "I have just the name for you. Pinocchio."

Figaro and Cleo didn't think much of the name, but the puppet nodded his head. He liked it!

Soon it was bedtime. Gepetto said goodnight to Cleo, and looked at Pinocchio, sitting on the bench. "Wouldn't it be nice," sighed the old man, "if he were a *real* boy!"

Gepetto had got into bed, and Figaro had curled up at his feet, when the old man remembered he hadn't opened the window. As he pulled it open, Gepetto saw a magnificent star.

"Oh, Figaro. Look!" he cried. "The wishing star." Gepetto clasped his hands together and wished hard. As he got back into bed, he said to Figaro, "I wished that my little Pinocchio might be a *real* boy."

Down below, Jiminy Cricket couldn't sleep, however hard he tried. He heard Gepetto talking about the star. Suddenly he sat up. A bright star was falling through the sky. The light got stronger and stronger. It came in through the window! Cautiously, Jiminy looked up. Standing by Gepetto's bench was the most beautiful Blue Fairy.

"Good Gepetto, you deserve to have your wish come true," she said. She waved her wand over Pinocchio. Pinocchio's strings dissolved, and he began to move.

"I can move," he cried. "I can talk! Am I a real boy?"

"No, Pinocchio, you are not," the Blue Fairy said. "To make Gepetto's wish come true will be entirely up to you. Prove yourself brave, truthful, unselfish, and some day you'll be a *real* boy."

Jiminy Cricket muttered, "That won't be easy."

"You must learn to choose between right and wrong," the Blue Fairy went on.

"But how will I know?" asked Pinocchio.

"Your conscience will tell you," the Blue Fairy told him.

Pinocchio was puzzled. "What are conscience?" he asked.

Jiminy was excited. "I'll tell you," he cried, parachuting down from his hiding place with his umbrella. "A conscience is that still, small voice…"

But he couldn't explain in a way Pinocchio could understand. The Blue Fairy laughed. "Would you like to be Pinocchio's conscience?" she asked Jiminy.

"Well, uh. . . well . . ." Jiminy stuttered, proud and embarrassed.

So it was agreed that Jiminy would take on this important job, and the Blue Fairy left while Jiminy and Pinocchio waved goodbye.

"It's my wish. It's come true!" Gepetto gasped when he discovered that Pinocchio was alive. He was so proud as he sent Pinocchio off to school bright and early in the morning. It was so early Jiminy Cricket was still asleep!

Lurking in an alley were two crooks, a fox called J. Worthington Foulfellow (though he liked to be called Honest John), and his crony, a big cat called Gideon. Honest John had been looking at a poster advertising Stromboli and his Marionette show. Just then they saw Pinocchio walking down the road on his way to school. Honest John stared.

"A little wooden boy!" he cried. "Look, Giddy, look . . . a live puppet without strings!"

Quickly he plotted with Gideon to trap Pinocchio and sell him to Stromboli, who would surely pay Honest John a lot of money for such a remarkable puppet.

The fox cunningly managed to trip Pinocchio up. As he dusted the puppet down, he started to talk about school. He told Pinocchio that there was a much easier road to success.

"I'm speaking, my boy, of the theatre. Bright lights . . . music . . . applause . . . *Fame!* Why," he finished, looking at the cat, "he's a natural born actor, eh, Giddy?" And so persuasive was Honest John, that Pinocchio agreed to go with him.

Jiminy Cricket woke up and went out looking for Pinocchio. He was horrified to see him with Honest John and Gideon. Jiminy knew they weren't to be trusted! In spite of all his arguments, Pinocchio insisted on staying with them.

"Oh, what'll I do?" sighed Jiminy, in despair. He turned back towards Gepetto's house. Then he stopped. "No," he said. "I'll go after him myself."

It took him a long time to find out where Pinocchio was and to catch up with him.

Pinocchio's song and dance act was a great success at Stromboli's marionette theatre. The little puppet was delighted by the applause, but Jiminy, who was watching, was worried. Perhaps Pinocchio should work in the theatre?

But later, when Stromboli was in his wagon counting the big
pile of money he had made, things changed. Stromboli would
not let Pinocchio go home! He wanted to tour the world, and
make his fortune with the puppet that had no strings. He flung
poor Pinocchio into a cage, and padlocked it.

"And when you grow old," he growled, waving an axe, "you
will make good *firewood*."

Poor Pinocchio. He sat in his cage miserably. If only he'd listened to Jiminy, his conscience! "Jiminy," he cried. Then he remembered that Jiminy had told him to whistle if he wanted him. He whistled at once. Jiminy came through a gap at the bottom of the door.

"What happened?" the cricket asked, seeing the cage. "What did he do to you?"

As Pinocchio told him the sad story, Jiminy worked on the padlock, but it was too strong for him.

A tear slid down Pinocchio's cheek. "I should have listened to you," he said sadly.

"No," Jiminy said. "I shouldn't have left you."

He looked out of the window of Stromboli's wagon, and saw a bright star. It was the Blue Fairy. Pinocchio started to tell her what had happened — but he began to exaggerate, to make the story sound better! As he talked, a ball of light formed on the end of his nose. Every time Pinocchio told a lie, his nose grew.

Then it started to sprout a small tree, which put out leaves and flowers!

"Oh! Oh! Look! . . ." wailed Pinocchio. "My nose! What's happened?"

The Blue Fairy looked at him seriously. "Perhaps you haven't been telling the truth, Pinocchio?"

Pinocchio knew he couldn't fool the Blue Fairy. "Please help me," he begged. "I'm awfully sorry. I'll never tell lies again."

"Very well," the fairy said. She raised her wand. And in a flash of light, Pinocchio's nose was restored to its right size, and he was freed from the cage. The fairy vanished.

Jiminy and Pinocchio jumped out of Stromboli's wagon, determined to go home to Gepetto as fast as they could.

Meanwhile, Honest John and Gideon were plotting more mischief. They were in the Red Lobster Inn, with a very shady character known as Coachman. He wanted boys — bad, disobedient boys — to take to Pleasure Island. Honest John was sure he and Gideon could find a few! And Coachman paid very well.

"There is no risk," Coachman reassured Honest John, with an evil grin on his face. "They *never* come back . . . as boys!"

The fox and the cat went off to look for bad boys.

Pinocchio and Jiminy were having a race to see who could
reach Gepetto's house first. Jiminy was ahead — when Honest
John and Gideon caught Pinocchio again! The fox listened
sympathetically as Pinocchio told him of the dreadful time
he'd had with Stromboli.

"You must be a nervous wreck!" the sly fox said. "There's only one cure. A holiday on Pleasure Island!" He made it sound so good that Pinocchio soon agreed to go with him, and it was not long before Honest John had bundled the puppet onto Coachman's coach.

It was full of boys, shouting and misbehaving.

It didn't take long to reach Pleasure Island, and the excited boys rushed off to enjoy all the delights. There was a carnival, there were tents for fighting, there were stalls where boys could eat as much as they could — there were all manner of things to delight bad boys!

It did not take long before Jiminy Cricket realized that Pinocchio was in trouble again. Once more the cricket tracked him down — but when he saw Pleasure Island, he was horrified. Everywhere he looked there were boys behaving badly, and there was no sign of Pinocchio. Where could he be?

"I don't like the look of this!" Jiminy muttered. "Pinocchio . . . Pinocchio . . . Where are you?"

At last Jiminy found Pinocchio playing with a dreadful boy called Lampwick. He had made Pinocchio sick by making him smoke a cigar and drink beer. Jiminy pleaded with Pinocchio to come away — but without success. Pinocchio was having too much fun! Jiminy was very angry and left Pinocchio.

"I've had enough of this!" he muttered. But when he got to the harbour, he found a gang of rough-looking men loading hundreds of donkeys onto boats. Coachman was watching.

"And what's your name?" he asked one donkey.

"Alexander," replied the animal. "I want to go home to my mama!"

"Quiet!" shouted Coachman. "You boys have had your fun — now you must pay for it!"

Jiminy was shocked. "So that's it," he gasped. "Oh, Pinocchio!"

He could not desert the puppet now. Jiminy rushed back to try to save him. "I hope I'm not too late!"

Pinocchio had been watching, very frightened, as Lampwick turned into a donkey. He felt very odd. What was the matter with his head? He put his hand up. His ears had turned into donkey's ears! Then a donkey's tail grew straight through the back of his trousers!

Jiminy shot through the door. He took one look at Pinocchio. "Quick, Pinoke — come on, quick, before you get any worse!"

They ran to the harbour wall, and dived into the water. It was a struggle to reach dry land again, and both Jiminy and Pinocchio were very wet and tired when they came ashore.

Once again they set off for Gepetto's house.

"Father! Father! I'm home!" Pinocchio shouted, running to the door. But it was shut, and in spite of all his banging, no one answered. There was nobody at home.

Pinocchio and Jiminy sat down miserably in the porch together. Jiminy tried to cheer Pinocchio up, but without success. Suddenly a beautiful white dove appeared. She dropped a paper in front of the pair. Jiminy picked it up. "It's about your father," he cried. "It says — he went looking for you, and — was swallowed by a whale!"

When Pinocchio heard what had happened, he was
determined to rescue Gepetto. So he and Jiminy set off once
again. When they reached the sea, Pinocchio tied his tail
round a large rock.

"Goodbye, Jiminy," he said.

"Goodbye?" Jiminy cried. "Oh, no, I'm going with you."

Together they jumped into the water. The rock was heavy
enough to carry Pinocchio down to the sea bed. He saw all
kinds of wonderful things, but none of the creatures wanted to
talk about Monstro.

It was true. Gepetto had been broken-hearted when
Pinocchio had not returned from school. He had waited and
waited, and then, afraid that something dreadful had
happened, he had taken Figaro and Cleo, and gone in search of
his son. They had been swallowed by the terrible whale,
Monstro.

Suddenly the water churned and boiled! Pinocchio found himself in the mouth of the giant whale! Then the mouth snapped shut.

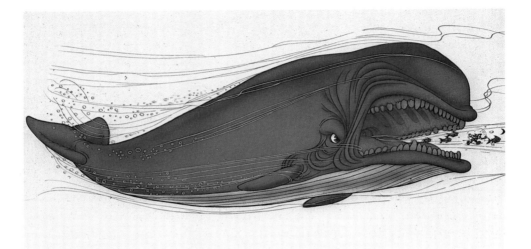

Deep inside the whale, Gepetto and Figaro were feeling very hungry. They were trying to catch a fish when a great wave of water went surging past. On top of it was Pinocchio!

How pleased they were to see each other again! Gepetto hugged Pinocchio hard, Figaro meowed, and Cleo jumped up and down. But how were they to get out? Gepetto had built a raft, but they needed to get Monstro to open his mouth again. Pinocchio had an idea.

"A fire!" he shouted. Quickly they built a fire. When they lit it, it made so much smoke that Monstro's insides were tickled, and he sneezed.

Jiminy Cricket had not been swallowed by the whale. He was outside, banging on Monstro's snout trying to get in. At last, when the whale sneezed, thick clouds of smoke came pouring out followed by Pinocchio, Gepetto, Figaro and Cleo, clinging to the raft.

The water was tossed everywhere. The little raft spun and whirled about, and the passengers could not hold on. They fell into the sea, and the angry Monstro smashed the raft into matchwood.

Gepetto had lost consciousness, and slowly and with difficulty Pinocchio towed him to the beach. Figaro, drenched and miserable, climbed out of the water, and Cleo, in her bowl, was flung onto the beach by a wave.

Jiminy Cricket had paddled ashore on a bottle. He saw Pinocchio lying on the beach. There was no sign of life. Some while later, Gepetto regained his senses. He found Figaro and Cleo, but when he reached Pinocchio, and saw that his son was dead, he wept bitterly. Grief-stricken, he carried Pinocchio home.

As Jiminy sat by a candle, crying as though his heart would break, he saw a bright light floating through the open window. From the centre stepped the Blue Fairy. She had promised Pinocchio that if he proved himself brave, truthful and unselfish, some day he would be a *real* boy.

"Awake, Pinocchio, awake!" she called, waving her wand.

Pinocchio sat up. He looked at Gepetto. "Father!" he cried. "I'm alive, see, and I'm a *real* boy!"

Gepetto could hardly believe it. He looked closely at Pinocchio. It was true! He swung Pinocchio round and round, he was so happy.

Then there was great rejoicing in Gepetto's house. Gepetto and Pinocchio danced, the clocks struck, the musical boxes played. Figaro even kissed Cleo, he was so pleased!

And to his great delight, Jiminy Cricket found that he had a big gold badge. It said *Official Conscience*. "Why . . . well, I'll be . . . " he stammered. "Solid gold, too." He rubbed it proudly and, standing on the window-ledge, looked out over the little village. "Thank you, Blue Fairy," he whispered.